Daniel Visits the Library

adapted by Maggie Testa

based on the screenplay "Calm for Storytime"

written by Wendy Harris

poses and layouts by Jason Fruchter

Ready-to-Read

Simon Spotlight

New York   London   Toronto   Sydney   New Delhi

SIMON SPOTLIGHT
An imprint of Simon & Schuster Children's Publishing Division
1230 Avenue of the Americas, New York, New York 10020
This Simon Spotlight edition August 2015
© 2015 The Fred Rogers Company
For information about special discounts for bulk purchases, please contact Simon & Schuster Special Sales at
1-866-506-1949 or business@simonandschuster.com.
Manufactured in the United States of America 1116 LAK
2 4 6 8 10 9 7 5 3 1
ISBN 978-1-4814-4174-2 (eBook)
ISBN 978-1-4814-9683-4 (prop)

"Trolley cannot go until you are calm," says Dad.

At last it is storytime!

We listen to the story.